Contents

For Nancy and all the Coldharbour "Tuesday Babies" — J.N.
For Karin and Ray, with love — C.R.

Text copyright © Jane Newberry 2020
Illustrations copyright © Carolina Rabei 2020
First published in Great Britain and in the USA in 2020 by Otter-Barry Books,
Little Orchard, Burley Gate, Herefordshire, HR1 3QS
www.otterbarrybooks.com

A catalogue record for this book is available from the British Library.

ISBN 978-1-910959-61-9

Illustrations created digitally

Set in Intro and Gotham

Printed in China

9 8 7 6 5 4 3 2 1

BIG GREEN CROCODILE

Rhymes by
Jane Newberry

•••

Pictures by
Carolina Rabei

Otter-Barry BOOKS

Spots and Stripes

Stripy tigers, stripy zebras,
stripy fishes in the sea.
Spotty dogs and spotty beetles,
spotty leopards running free....

In the jungle stripes can hide you,
in the desert spots don't show.
All the animals are hiding
till they jump out
and say...

BOO!!

LET'S PLAY – JUNGLE!
For the stripy animals, pass
your fingers in front of your eyes.
Make 'spots' in the air with your finger-tips,
up for dogs, down low for beetles, and move
your fingers from left to right for leopards.
Cover your eyes for 'hiding', and make
the 'BOO' a big surprise!

Five Buzzy Bees

High five, low five!
Five little buzzy bees buzzing in a hive,
up to the mountain, down to the sea.
Up to my head,
down to my knee.

Bzzzzz

High five, low five!
Five little buzzy bees buzzing in a hive.

**LET'S PLAY –
BUZZY BEE!**
Do a 'high five' with the
child, as high as they can
reach, and 'low five' down on
the floor. Make 'buzzy bees'
with your fingers, moving
your arms up and down.

LET'S PLAY - CAMEL!
Sit the child on your knees
and jog them up and down.
Let the 'camel-rider' fall
GENTLY to the floor
on the word 'bump'.

My Camel

I'm on my camel
out in the desert,
feeling so high and grand.
Then my camel sneezes
and falls on his kneezes...
and I go down

BUMP

in the sand!

ACHOO!

9

Monster March

How shall we go? What do you say?
Plodding along like a monster – Hey!
Roar – er... roar – er!
Every day is a monster day.

How shall we go? What do you say?
Rolling along like a robot – Hey!
Bleep tikka bleep... bleep tikka bleep!
Every day is a robot day.

How shall we go? What do you say?
Hopping along like a frog – Hey!
Rebbit – croak... rebbit – croak!
Every day is a frog day.

**LET'S PLAY –
MARCHING!**
Stand up and act out
plodding, rolling, hopping.
Try 'waddling along like
a duck, quack!' or add
your own ideas.

LET'S PLAY – CLOWN!
With babies, swop 'stretch right up/flop right down' for 'hands go up and hands go down', holding their hands. Help them to find their nose (line 6). Older children will enjoy shaking, wobbling, stretching up and flopping down to the ground.

Wibble-Wobble Clown

Wibble wobble, wibble wobble,
Wibble-Wobble Clown,
Stretch right UP and flop right DOWN!
Wibble wobble, wibble wobble,
what do you suppose?
Wibble-Wobble Clown has a big red NOSE.
Wibble wobble, wibble wobble,
Wibble-Wobble Clown,
Stretch right UP and...

flop right DOWN!

11

Hungry Horse

Clop, clop, clopetty clop,
down the road and into the shop.
Buy him a carrot and home we pop.
Clop, clop, clopetty clop!

LET'S PLAY – HORSE!
Jog the child or baby on your lap.
You can repeat, getting faster
each time. Or sit opposite the
child on the floor and clap for
the 'clops' (1,2,3,4) or beat
two wooden spoons.

Here Comes the Farmer

Here comes the farmer,
driving the tractor,
digger, digger, digger, digger,
digger, digger, dig, with
hay for the horses,
cattle-cake for cows and
mash for the little pink pig!

Squeak!

Oink, oink, oink, oink, squeak, squeak, squeak.
Here's mash for the little pink pig!

mooo!

LET'S PLAY – FARM!
Sit the baby or child on
your lap, facing you, and
jog your knees to the
rhythm of the words.
Let the 'oinks' be grunty
and low and the 'squeaks'
be squeaky and high.

Moon Rocket

Jump into the rocket,
we're going to the moon.
Once around the galaxy
and be back soon.
Ready for the take-off...
Listen for the boom...

and ZoooooOM!

Tap the Tree

With my stick I tap the tree
with a tap tap, tap tap, tap tap, tap.
But the tree says,
"Who's that tapping on me?"
So I clap clap, clap clap,
clap
clap,
CLAP!

TAP!

LET'S PLAY – TREE!
It's lovely to do this rhyme
outside with a real stick
on a real tree. Indoors you
could tap two wooden
spoons together.

Plane Spotting

**LET'S PLAY –
AEROPLANE!**
This is a calming-down
rhyme. Lie on the floor
and point up to the sky.
It's even better outdoors
where you may see
real aeroplanes.

Here I lie,
looking at the sky,
watching all the aeroplanes
as they fly...

Taking all the people
far, far away,
taking all the people
on a holiday...

Where do they holiday?
Where do they go?
Where do they fly to?
I don't know.

The Queen Comes to Tea

The Queen comes to tea.
What shall we make?
Ice-cream, cookies and chocolate cake!

Off on a picnic.
What shall we take?
Ice-cream, cookies and chocolate cake!

Somebody's birthday?
What shall we bake?
ICE-CREAM, COOKIES
AND CHOCOLATE CAKE!

Yum!

**LET'S PLAY –
TEA PARTY!**
Place hands facing
upwards on your head for
the queen's crown. Clap
for the last line of each
verse, getting really loud
on the last one.

Brontosaurus Ride

Bibb-ly bobb-ly, bibb-ly bobb-ly
Brontosaurus ride.
Bibb-ly bobb-ly, up and down,
bibb-ly bobb-ly, side to side.
Bibb-ly bobb-ly, bibb-ly bobb-ly, bobb-ly up to the TOP!
Bibb-ly bobb-ly, Brontosaurus,
SLOWER AND SLOWER...
and STOP.

**LET'S PLAY –
BRONTOSAURUS!**
You can do this rhyme with the child
riding on your shoulders, or jogging/
riding on your lap. Older children
can straddle the back of a willing
grown-up on all fours!

Tickle Beetle

Tickle Beetle runs round your tummy...
Tickle Beetle jumps on your nose.
Tickle Beetle runs all down your leg
and jumps up and down on your toes.
Up and down, up and down.
He jumps up and down on your toes.

LET'S PLAY – BEETLE!
Create a nice sensory experience by wiggling your fingers and tickling as much or as little as your baby or child likes. Vary your voice with high and low tones – as speech develops, the baby will copy you.

Fish Tales

Fishy in the ocean,
Fishy in the sea,
Fishy diving in the surf,
Splish, splash - wheeee!

Fishy in the rock pool,
Fishy swimming free.
Fishy dives beneath the weed...
Can't catch ME!

Fishy in the bathtub,
Fishy swim to me.
Out you jump
with a 1... 2... 3!

LET'S PLAY - FISH!
This rhyme helps with getting out of the bath. Do the actions for verse 1 and 2 with your hands in the bath. For verse 3 hold your hands and the towel out, as you say 1,2,3!

Jumping Panda

Round and round goes Panda,
round and round some more...

Jump-ing Panda! Jump-ing Panda!
Jumping on the floor.

Sleepy Panda, sleepy Panda,
softly stroke his head.

Naughty Panda! Naughty Panda!
Jumping on the bed!

LET'S PLAY – PANDA!
For babies, sit them
on your lap and lift them up
for 'jumping panda'. Older
children can act out the
verses, walking in a circle/
rolling, jumping, lying down to
be stroked – and jumping up
for last verse.

Big Green Crocodile

A great big green crocodile lay down for a nap.
I lay down beside him until he went...SNAP!
A great big brown lion lay down on the floor.
I lay down beside him until he went...ROAR!
A small furry teddy lay down with a yawn.
I lay down beside him and slept until dawn.

**LET'S PLAY –
BEDTIME!**

As each creature lies down,
lie down on the floor (or bed),
then sit up for 'snap' and
'roar'. For the last verse,
do a big yawn with the child
and lie down quietly.